There Is No Escape.
Stories by Samantha Sewell

Published by Mother Mercury
Copyright © 2023 by Samantha Sewell
ISBN: 978-1-7396393-3-4

All rights reserved. No part of this publication may be reproduced, stored in a retrieval system or transmited in any form or by any means, electronic, mechanical, photocopying, recording or otherwise without the prior permission of the publisher or in accordance with the provisions of the Copyright, Designs and Patents Act 1988 or under the terms of any licence permitting limited copying issued by the Copyright Licensing Agency.

This book is a work of fiction. Names, characters, places, and incidents, either are products of the author's imagination or are used fictitiously. Any resemblance to actual events or locales or persons, living or dead, is entirely coincidental.

A CIP record for this book is available from the Library of Congres.

Cover Design: Samantha Sewell & Christian Jarod Vitug

www.despairyemighty.com/mother-mercury • www.samanthasewell.com

For Mom, Dad, and Rocky

Contents

Preface: Someone   1

Raquel / The Idea of Crying   3

Nadine   19

Pip   29

Joany   45

Willie   53

Felix & Emma   65

Me and You (and Everyone Else)   79

Preface
Someone

Somewhere right now, someone

is lying to their dentist, ordering water shoes, stealing toilet paper from their parents, shaping their pubic hair into a triangle, overfeeding the ducks, ignoring their grandparent, becoming irrelevant, laughing at the moon, flirting with their neighbor, pulling at their eyelashes, dancing in a dream underwater and not enjoying it, worrying about lunch with their boring best friend, drowning out sex noises with a French horn, provoking their ex, rolling in the grass, looking for the entrance, rearranging their collection of Troll dolls, crushing the ego of a drunk, singing really well in the shower, bathing in the sun (fully clothed), running the wrong way on a treadmill, waiting for their parents to die, whispering dirty jokes in a shopping mall, cursing their unborn child, curling up on their kitchen floor, comparing

State Farm to Geico, chain-smoking cigarettes, holding in their pee, chaperoning the elderly, crying against their will, hallucinating in a minivan, hanging upside-down, denying the Holocaust, flipping their pillow to the cold side.

Somewhere, right now, someone is searching for an escape.

Raquel / The Idea of Crying

The idea of crying has become very glamorous to Raquel. It seems only wealthy people at royal funerals or teenagers on social media are granted the privilege. Often now, something sad happens, and she becomes too excited to cry. Then she doesn't cry.

Lately, she's been experimenting with fabricating events worthy of a cry, which is not as simple as imagining her brother's funeral; that is too obvious—a layman's cry. Any event that demands tears in such a torpid state produces few (if any at all) for those old enough to have fallen out of love with the world. Most adults need somewhere safe to hide too. But even in hiding, Raquel is unable to succeed.

Yesterday was a big day in pursuit of tears. She fantasized about Vito, her former neighbor, a very tall and brutal man, locking her away in his room and using her like a rag doll. She imagined her own piercing screams—the way her body writhes when he strikes her, the burns on her wrists from the rope, keeping her limbs tied together.

But Vito has a mole on his lower lip that dances when he comes. It makes her sorry—an otherwise good-looking man tormented by his own mole. His woes no bigger than half a square inch yet rectified only in vain. Maybe if he were adequately insured, he could visit a doctor. He wouldn't need to torture girls like Raquel. But the tech start-up he works for has yet to set up a health care plan, and even when they do, the likelihood of coverage for cosmetic surgeries is low. So, Vito spends his life watching others watch his mole while in conversation. And every time the homely woman at his local drug store asks, "How are you today, sir?" his ears burn with rage in the moments thereafter, when he has to sort out whether she is inquiring with him, the man, or the mole.

After Vito came the plane crash. Raquel imagined a storm tossing her around, the passengers beside her, frightened and holding onto their seats for dear life, while the flight attendants sit stoic and unaffected, dedicated to their work, trained not to panic in the event of a crash. If they panic, we all panic.

Raquel contemplates who to call in her final moments. Somehow, she gets through to her mother by phone, only to have the line drop after "I love—". Now her mother will never know what she loved. With no one listening, it will be as though she never loved. Even when Raquel looks left for a witness, there is no one paying attention.

The woman beside her hugs a newborn against her chest as she mutters to God, while two strangers one row over swap confessions, hoping to bypass hell.

"When I was four, I swore I didn't call the nanny a bitch, but…"

"Sometimes, I'd press Ken Barbie between my thighs, but…"

And even as the outside of the plane catches fire, plummeting toward the Atlantic, none of this makes Raquel want to cry. In fact, she wants to yell, "No buts! It's fine! That's normal! Excuse me, miss? There is no God."

In Raquel's last attempt to cry she got creative. Instead of being the victim of a tragedy outside of her control, she made herself the useless, guilty bystander to another's tragedy. She pictured the M9 bus delayed at the Centre Street stop; her, passing by, late for Pilates with Clarissa, who is her favorite instructor, who is always commenting on her posture, who is always telling her, "Surely you were a ballerina in a past life." As she rushes by, a masked man enters the bus. She notices him, but she continues. She tells herself it's a fad. She's not up to date on the latest fashion trends. It could be a popular look among youths.

Then, she hears the doors of the bus barricade shut; she hears him yelling and the passengers crying, and she realizes the ski mask is not a fashion statement. But she is asking him to kill her if she turns around to help. So, she keeps walking. She has to save herself. It's over within seconds. Twenty-two fatalities, even the murderer.

Later, at home, Raquel watches the news—a blurry clip from inside the bus—a glimpse of his eyes through the mask, two nuns, ten-year-old twin boys. Sets of twos, like Noah's ark if Noah were suicidal and white and still living at home and angry at the world, and failed by our modern-day educational system, which does not appreciate woodshop the way it used to. As Raquel watches the news, she rubs her back. She pulled a muscle in Pilates. Clarissa had a sub. She should have checked the schedule.

"Raquel. What is wrong with you?" asks her mother. "There are children starving in Africa."

"Huh?" Raquel looks down at her soggy cereal bowl.

In twenty-eight years of life, she's never found an argument against the starving African children. Once she thought she came close. "There are children starving in America too," but this only debunked the narrow focus of food insecurity. She still had to finish her plate.

Raquel picks at her cereal. There is no point. Food is just energy. And energy for what?

Two years ago, Raquel moved back into her childhood home. She had been working as a personal assistant in "entertainment," and one day her boss was admonishing her about his poodles defecating in the shower. The next day her parents were dying, and she needed to fly home. This was not the first boss to turn Raquel into a timid fabulist. Authority did not agree with her.

In an effort to preserve her pride, Raquel convinced herself that her parents were dying. She claimed she had seen a totter in her mother's gait last Christmas; that her walk had turned into a waddle, as if her toes were flexing away from a soaking wet carpet. This new walk was reminiscent of the way Raquel's grandmother used to walk. It could only mean that her mother was dying, and probably her father too. So, she returned home, defiantly designating herself as their caretaker.

Really, these were just early, early signs of the eventual end. There were never any dying parents to care for, and there are still no dying parents to care for. There are only middle-aged bodies traipsing around, still dexterous enough to open their pickle jars and sane enough to balance their checkbooks.

"I'm going to put a load in. Anything you'd like to add?" her mother asks, grabbing Raquel's milky bowl and rinsing it in the sink.

"On the vanity," Raquel sighs.

Raquel's mother heads off to her childhood bedroom.

"Thanks!" Raquel yells, an afterthought. She listens for the laundry to start. Her mother shuffles around. There's a thump, and then a thud. She is busy with something else. "Do you need help?" Raquel asks. A few moments pass. "Mom?"

"It's a mess in here. I'm just tidying up."

"Oh...sorry."

"Which one's the dirty pile?"

"The vanity! The one on the vanity!" Raquel waits. "Do you see—

"Found it."

After a minute or so, the laundry starts, but her mother doesn't return.

Raquel downs the rest of her coffee, which is now cold in the icy indoor air. Her parents never use the heater. Growing up, if she and her brother were ever cold, they were told to add a layer. The reverse of this did not apply in the summer. They were not one of those naked families, always running around in their underwear. As soon as the weather hit seventy, the air conditioning was on. Frugality and repression dictated the temperature of their home; seventy degrees was the only time the weather had a say, but this was just to save each of them from the other's nudity.

"What are you doing now?" Raquel yells. "Mom? Mom!"

"I'm using the bathroom! Jeez. Would you like to join?"

"Sorry," Raquel deflates. "Sorry," she whispers.

Her parents are never going to tell her she is unneeded, or unwanted, but after two years of sleeping in a twin bed and using her mother's credit card, Raquel is starting to feel a little in the way.

Typically, a parent's obligation is to make their child feel "at home." But home is no longer *home*, and Raquel is not a child. So, instead, she wanders around the house each day in her gray pajamas and matching gray slippers, offering help in the kitchen, in the office, in her parents' bedroom, and now apparently even in the bathroom. Sometimes her father asks her to reorganize his collection of telephone bills from the 1990s, claiming it's about time he digitized things. But he is only really placating her. It wasn't supposed to be like this when she moved home. She was supposed to add value.

Now she waits around for their impotence.

It's only a matter of time until the neighbors become suspicious of her. Raquel imagines a couple more years going by, her parents remaining in good health, and Rita, next door, commenting on how sprightly they are, even in their old age. "That's because I take very good care of them. Driving them to doctors' appointments, separating their medicine, cooking dinner, reorganizing the hall closet, etcetera, etcetera," Raquel would say. She imagines Rita winking at her as if to initiate her into the club of star children.

But then, with each passing year, Rita would start to notice that neither of them has died yet. She would comment on their agelessness. And Raquel would say, "Yes, yes. That's because I take very good care of them. Driving them to doctors' appointments, separating their medicine, cooking dinner, reorganizing the hall closet, etcetera, etcetera." And Rita would wink again, resubscribing her into the club of star children.

But at some point, her parents would actually begin to age. And Rita would see that what she once thought was agelessness was really just middle age, and what she once thought was years of Raquel's selfless servitude to them was really just Raquel moving home in her late twenties due to a dreadful indecision over how to proceed with life. Then she would no longer belong in the club of star children.

The front door swings open. Raquel jolts. Her father enters, whistling a tune he's made up.

"Well, good morning to you," he says. "I have returned two sweaters, deposited a check, filled three prescriptions, and scraped the sidewalk clear of snow. And it's only," he checks his watch. "Ten past ten," her father beams. "What have you been up to Bubaloo?" he asks.

Raquel watches him take off his coat. Their lives are not well-aligned. His unwavering tranquility is maddening. Raquel looks down, trying to conceal an involuntary animosity of which he is not deserving.

"I've been…helping mom with the laundry," Raquel says, heading toward the sink to rinse her coffee mug.

"Oh, that reminds me—where is your mother? You're not going to believe who I ran into."

"Bathroom."

"Honey?" her father yells. "Hon!" He heads toward the bathroom.

"Yes? I'm in the bathroom!" her mother yells back.

"Honey, listen to this; you're not going to believe who I just ran into."

"Okay, can't it wait until I'm out of the bathroom?"

"Real quick. I'll just tell you through the door."

Raquel listens from the kitchen sink.

"It was Fanny Wood's mom. Fanny Woods? Is that right? She went to middle school with Raquel. Remember? With the dad who up and left for London with the nanny? It was the mother. Celine. Fanny Wood's mother," Raquel's father repeats this several times. It's proving difficult to communicate through the bathroom door.

Celine was at Target when Raquel's father was returning his sweaters. Celine was returning Fanny's, apparently, unused breast pump. Fanny had her first kid at twenty years old. This was somewhat of a statistical anomaly, as she had been menstruating already for eleven years. The neighborhood expected a teen pregnancy.

While everyone else was away at college, "finding themselves," and judging Fanny for trading college for motherhood, Fanny was taking prenatal vitamins, and shopping for onesies and bottles and teddies, and rubbing cocoa butter on her belly, and finally, for once in her life, feeling at peace, like this was exactly the role she always wanted. When everyone graduated, Fanny was onto her second child, raking in money from her million-plus following on Instagram, while her former peers moved home to spend eight hours a day belaboring over cover letters for entry-level jobs.

"She has three kids now. Same father," Celine had barked in the "Returns and Exchanges" line. "He's a wonderful dad," she said. "A wonderful dad," she felt the need to repeat.

After Celine's husband left her, Raquel's father used to see her downtown at the local pubs. Sometimes he would drink next to her, and she would flirt with him until his buddies showed up. He was always polite but reserved. He entertained her for a respectable amount of time, then raised his glass and excused himself, freeing the chair beside her for someone inevitably less kind. Celine knew Raquel's mother well from their overlapping chaperone duties on select middle school field trips. The flirting was all in good fun. Raquel's father was just a buffer for the rest of her evening.

"Anyway, three kiddos. No way that wasn't a heavily used pump in there. Right?" her father yells through the bathroom door.

"Dad!" Raquel joins her father in the hall outside the bathroom.

"What?" he turns to her, hands tossed into the air, "I would question any item. It's not my fault it was a breast pump!"

"Really? So, if it was, I don't know, like a water bottle, you'd assume she had used it a bunch before returning it?"

"Well, yes, perhaps a few times. Don't you think that's how most people decide they don't want the thing they bought before they head back to return it? But Bubby, you're not getting my point. She has three kiddos now, all older than nursing age, I would presume. There's no way she didn't use that puppy for at least a few years."

"Ew!" Raquel shudders.

"What?"

"Don't call it a puppy."

"Excuse me? Can you two have this conversation anywhere else?" Raquel's mother yells from beyond the bathroom door.

"How 'bout I call it a pump-y?" Raquel's father whispers, chuckling. He gestures for them to exit the hall and continue the conversation elsewhere, but Raquel doesn't move.

She is too fixated on how pronounced his crow's feet have become—a lifetime of jokes like these compressed at the corners. She can tell this one will keep him going for the rest of the day, into the night even. In bed later, he'll reach over to shut off the lamp and let out a giggle in the dark before drifting off to sleep. Retired. Content. He did all the things he was supposed to do—career, sex, wife, sex, kids, sex, travel, sex. Now he floats around running errands. Raquel doesn't know whether she envies his wrinkles or whether she hates them. Or whether she hates him.

"You know what? It's fine! I think the conversation ended!" Raquel shouts toward her mother. She hears the toilet flush. "I'm going for a walk." She slides past her father before the abandonment registers on his face.

"Something I said?" he calls after her. His voice cracks and rolls toward his throat.

It makes her limbs numb and watery. If time were a physical substance, Raquel would feel her pores absorbing it, consuming the awareness that she, and her parents, and everyone else are all, slowly, crawling toward the end.

In this moment, Raquel wants to run back over to her father and squeeze him the way she used to when he'd return home from work. When she'd drop anything just to hug his legs. The other day she was trying to remember at what age she stopped doing that. And why! Why? Why would she ever stop hugging him?

He hasn't moved from the hall yet, and as Raquel heads for the door, she knows it isn't too late. She can still turn around and call out to him.

I'm sorry! I love you! I'm sorry! I'm sorry! It's only a walk, okay? Nothing to do with you, okay? Please, please, please don't die while I'm gone, okay? Mom, you too, okay? I love you both, okay?

But the momentum of such a futile morning propels her out into the frosty air. She accidentally slams the door on the way out instead.

* * *

The only time Raquel ever felt at home while growing up was on a walk. She never liked the noise of the city. She never took to the aggression of its inhabitants the way transplants did, smiling at a middle finger and calling it "refreshing." She used to walk blocks and blocks just to shake away the pressure she felt upon stepping outside. However, her remedy for relief was flawed in its circularity.

There was no escaping. She was like a hamster on a wheel, moving as fast as she could but always stuck in one place.

From a young age, she dreamt of running away to California, even though she had very little idea of what California was actually like. She just knew it was far, far away. Raquel even made it to Los Angeles after college. This was where she spent most of her 20s. She wanted to be an actress. She had one national commercial and a few short films, then she quit.

Now, she walks the same streets she always walked, watching her footsteps until it grows dark. Typically, these walks do not have a destination, or an end point, or a pit stop of any kind.

On this walk, however, Raquel ends up at Target.

"Do you know where I can find, uh, baby items?" Raquel asks the employee posted by the entrance.

"Infant care is aisle fourteen," he says.

"Infant care," Raquel mutters, correcting herself.

At aisle fourteen, Raquel stops before the breast pumps. She surveys the many kinds, the smiling mothers holding sleeping newborns on the packaging. No matter the brand, every single mother is smiling, and every single newborn is sleeping. They are both so happy. Only one brand has a dad on the box. He smiles too, his hands placed on both of the mother's shoulders. It should be nice to see a father included, but it isn't. It's creepy. It looks like he's forcing the mother to smile, his grip on her shoulders a threat rather than a comfort. Poor dad.

The dads are left out. But, then again, they don't have to milk themselves. If men breast fed, these pumps would be everywhere—a section at Pep Boys, two aisles in Home Depot. If men breast fed there would never, ever be a woman on the packaging. There wouldn't even be a baby. It would just be a man with outrageously large pecks, holding a breast pump in front of his chest like a football. Men everywhere would start pumping themselves nonstop. They'd be tossing frisbees in the park, shirtless, with a pump hanging from their nipples. The NBA would rewrite the rules, allowing actively breast-pumping players three free throws rather than two. Hot dog eating contests would be replaced by breast-pumping contests. The men would forget entirely that the pumping served a purpose. The babies would starve.

Thank God men don't breast feed. Thank God God made mothers the cows. Perhaps it isn't easy on the mothers, but it's worked well for the babies thus far.

There is never another time when a baby is more in need of its mother than during infancy. It cannot speak, it cannot walk, it cannot feed itself. It can only cry. And the mother can't stand the crying, so she spends every moment she can pursuing ways to stop it. This relationship is easy at first, but over time, the baby becomes a child, and then a teenager, and then an adult, and the crying becomes less and less necessary. The distance between parent and child grows wider and wider in the years after the breast pump is tossed, until one day everything flips, and the mother becomes the one in need. She spends her life showing infants how to care so as to be replaced by progeny in old age.

To care and then to be cared for. This is understood even outside of humanity. This dynamic appears simple when one is needing and the other is providing, but nobody speaks of the space in between. When neither needs anything from the other. With no one crying, and no one needing, the water turns murky. The ground beneath the mother and child trembles. Suddenly, there is new space to navigate. It's disruptive, but at least there is something to pivot off of.

What, then, becomes of the father and the child? When there isn't much ground underneath at the start, where do they go?

One of the boxes is slightly ripped, tearing open the face of a cardboard mother. Raquel reaches out. She tucks the ripped piece in so that the face is slightly more intact. Then, she heads for the checkout.

On her way home, Raquel passes the private pre-school that used to be a boxing gym, the bank that used to be a bakery. She counts all the buildings that used to be something else—illegitimate and underfunded church basements, sports centers, and community colleges where she learned to sing, and swim, and dance. It seems overnight everything changed. Her singing instructor moved to New Jersey, and then Raquel stopped hugging her father's legs.

But even after all this change, there was still a familiarity with the neighborhood. For a little while, it still felt like home. Raquel could walk by the bank and yearn for the bakery. She could remember the crunch their baguettes made when she bit into the center. More recently, though, the bank didn't look like it could have ever adequately housed a bakery. The dimensions seemed off—implausible. It looked like it could have only ever been a bank. It was around this time that the idea of crying became very glamorous to Raquel.

"Dad!" Raquel yells as she enters the apartment. She can hear the laundry still running. Her coffee mug has been thoroughly washed and now dries beside the sink. "Dad?" Raquel's heart skips.

"He's taking a nap," her mother's faint voice travels from the office.

Raquel kicks off her shoes. She heads toward her parents' bedroom. She can hear her father's snores from beyond the door. Slowly, she enters the room, stopping just inches above him.

"Dad," she whispers. She reaches out and touches his arm.

"Mm," he twitches awake, looking up at her, a flash of worry preceding annoyance.

"I got the pump," Raquel lifts Fanny's boxed breast pump from beneath her armpit. "Let's see how used it really is."

Nadine

I am French!

Nadine has three teeth.

Excuse me?

She is small, dirty, and kissed by the sun.

I am from Brussels!

On her head rests a small visor, which shields her from any unwanted disturbance.

Brussels, France!

Nadine pushes a little shopping cart in front of her. She stops by an overpriced fuchsia armoire when she sees the young lady near the holiday trinkets. She is astounded, joyous. Those watching would assume she'd spotted a long-lost friend.

She gasps loud enough to grab the girl's attention. *Your legs!* she points.

The girl looks down at her legs.

Nadine continues, *They are so incredibly long. Your proportions are so, so good my dear.*

Nadine possesses a vibrance for life lost among most. Her grin fills her whole face. It is the kind of smile that suggests Nadine is swimming while others are walking.

The girl recognizes this otherworldliness. She wants to turn away in dismissal, but there is a wrench in her gut that is uncompromising. It pulls her in. It makes the walls melt. Surrounding shoppers blur and sink into the floor. She and Nadine become the only two in the store. The girl holds onto Nadine, balancing her brightness, trying to bridge the gap between their two worlds.

As she tracks down Nadine's body, noting the oily, unkempt hair and the dirt beneath her fingernails, she soon recognizes her late grandmother—her father's mother—in Nadine's posture: the way she stands scrunched and small, yet no less determined to be seen. An enduring throb swells in her throat, which the girl carefully conceals.

When she is able to stay afloat, she and Nadine set off for a swim.

I am French, Nadine repeats.

The girl hesitates. *Oh, yeah?*

Nadine nods, proudly.

Where in France are you from?

Brussels. From Brussels, France.

Wow! The girl wonders if this is a real place in France. Brussels, France? Belgium? Could be a different Brussels. Could be a Brussels based in France.

Momentarily, the girl has forgotten she is talking to Nadine. She must disregard her own logic to accept Nadine's, which is to understand Brussels as a place within the country of France. They are swimming. It is Nadine's world. Brussels is in France.

Nadine scans the girl's legs again. She is in heaven. *The proportion!* she says.

My proportion?

Oh, yes! Nadine steps closer. *Listen,* she goes on, *it is all about the proportion. Do you know?*

I don't know . . . says the girl.

All about the proportion. Because, if you think about when you try on a big hat, you can never do this while you are sitting. Because, because—

Because of your proportions?

Yes, exactly! Nadine points at the girl the way her late grandfather—her mother's father—used to when he spoke of black bears sorting through the neighbor's trash. It's the same way her mother now points at her when she remembers what she's forgotten. The same way she will sometimes point at her cat, Lesley, when he gets close to knocking the water glass off her nightstand.

You! Your legs are so, so long. But your body is smaller. It's perfect! Just perfect. Nadine shakes her head over the proportional gold mine she's stumbled upon.

The girl notices that her French accent weaves in and out, occasionally overtaken by an American one.

How tall are you, darling?

About five-foot-six. I don't know, um, what that is in centimeters.

It is so tall! See, I am just one fifty-seven and a half. I think it is, eh, four inches less.

The girl nods. Nadine is certainly closer to five feet than five-two, but it seems like height is a different kind of thing in Nadine's world. It has more to do with character than measurement.

You understand what I am saying, yes? With the proportions? They are so, so important because if you think about when you try on a big hat—if you are sitting you cannot see. You need to see the proportions, otherwise, it will look, you know. You have to stand so that you can see—

The proportions, the girl affirms, and Nadine glows. They are gliding across water now.

Yes! Exactly. The proportions! Because if I put on a big hat, and I am sitting, then I don't see—I am so small underneath. And then, if I go outside, everyone will be running away from me! Nadine soars over rolling waves.

The girl imagines a hoard of people screaming and sprinting down the street, followed by five-two Nadine in a giant yellow sun hat (the terror!). The girl nods.

Nadine's eyes widen and she nods too. *Uh-huh. You see?* she asks.

Yes.

Yes! Nadine tosses her bony fist in the air. *It's all about the proportion.*

Nadine starts away, satisfied, but then she decides she isn't finished. *Oh! And you know, my dear, what you have to do is, is, you have to go now, and you have to find a wall, a, you know, a blank wall. Nothing behind it. And then, then you have to get naked.*

Naked?

Yes! Oh, yes, Nadine laughs as though she understands how ridiculous it sounds.

The girl imagines herself naked, fully naked, in front of a blank wall.

And then, Nadine proceeds, *then you have to have someone trace you, trace your body. And then you will see.*

What will I see?

Well, your proportions of course!

Of course. The girl thinks. My proportions.

It's just so... Nadine continues, *it's really so you can see, you really see, then, with the proportion, you see all of it. And you will see it's so—*

What? Horrendous?

Nadine jumps, placing one hand on her cart and the other on her heart.

The girl's friend chimes in. She had been coasting just beneath Nadine's radar, sitting in a $340 chair, watching a YouTube video, a little less invested in Nadine's appreciation for proportions. The friend seems irritated. In Nadine's world, this would make her about four-five (one hundred and thirty-five centimeters).

Yes, um, horrendous, Nadine shakes her head, thrown off by the friend. She reaches up to adjust her sun visor and returns to her version of clarity. *But no!* she says. *So, so beautiful too. It's beautiful.*

Beautiful? the girl asks.

Oh, yes. You will see, Nadine begins to push her shopping cart away, then stops again, admiring the girl's proportions one final time. *Do you see? It's all about the proportion.*

Yes. Okay. I see, says the girl.

Nadine stands up a little straighter, as though a weight has been lifted off of her. Finally. She's been waiting for someone to share in her regard for proportions, searching endlessly for anyone on this plane to understand. Now that she has found someone, she can return home. She can rest.

Of course, Nadine doesn't leave just yet. She belabors the concept of trying on large hats for a little while, warning the girl of the pitfalls of doing it seated. And the girl's investment in Nadine wavers as she becomes repetitive. But then, the girl remembers how much quicker she had lost patience for her own grandmother and her own grandfather when they had begun repeating themselves.

So, for them, she stays for Nadine. She leaves Nadine's moment of departure entirely up to Nadine. It is a tenuous effort to redeem herself, to undo the past, but it is not devoid of pure intention. The girl hopes, too, that Nadine will leave the furniture store with the feeling that someone was there for her.

Unfortunately, the girl will never know completely what staying to listen will mean for Nadine. And Nadine will never know what it will mean for the girl. Eventually, they will part, and it is possible that Nadine will swim on with no recollection of the interaction, while the girl will walk away without an ounce of redemption. Nadine will search for another soul housed in perfect proportions, and the girl will go on just as wrecked over the shortcomings of her own love for those who had dropped off (into a world akin to Nadine's).

What is your name? the girl asks.

Nadine. I am Nadine. But, my dear, Nadine points toward the girl. *Remember about the proportions, okay?* Nadine rolls her cart away.

The girl smiles as Nadine leaves. Then, she turns to her friend, who is relieved that Nadine is gone. The friend whispers, *Now all I can think about is Nadine tracing your naked body along a blank wall.*

The girl chuckles, but her heart is achy.

As the friend finishes her YouTube video, the girl listens to Nadine striking up a conversation with the furniture store owner by the entrance. She can tell he is trying to shoo her away.

The girl leaves the shop mourning the absence of Nadine. Except Nadine is a stranger. Can one really mourn the absence of a stranger?

On the ride home, the girl's friend rates the ex-boyfriend of her boyfriend's ex-girlfriend, but the girl is distracted. Her friend seems shorter than before. The steering wheel is far too big for her.

I miss Nadine, the girl admits.

Yeah? the friend laughs. *She was so weird.*

The sun is gone when they return to the girl's childhood home. The girl has grown distant. Her color is gone. Her breath is hollow. The friend tilts toward her like she understands; she squeezes the girl's hand.

Sorry, the friend says. *I wasn't thinking.*

When they go inside, the friend pushes aside care packages and deli platters leftover from the grandfather's recent wake. She helps the girl undress, laying her out against the cool, white cement wall in the basement.

Halfway through, the girl can feel her face becoming wet, although her eyes are dry. The tears are falling from the ceiling.

When her friend finishes tracing, the two of them step back from the wall. In the pitch black of the basement, a thin trail of streetlight gives way to a wobbly silhouette.

Pip

A red onion does not rot easily. It takes a long time.

In the earliest stage, the rot begins in one small spot. But this is easy to chop off as long as you are careful not to snip your finger. When the rot really takes over, it does so from the outside first. The external layers start to wilt. Then, the whitish-green mold spreads. But even these moldy layers are easy to peel away toward a fresh center. It takes a long time for the entire onion to soil. It takes a lot of effort to neglect it for so long. Unless there is a lack of care. If you have no reason to care, letting it decay is no trouble at all.

***

Pip left the front door unlocked for Oona because she would likely still be bathing. At some point toward the end of her shower, she could hear the door rattle the walls. Oona's timing was fortuitous. Pip was just finishing up The Long Shower.

The Long Shower always ends down on her knees, the shower head spitting water onto her face like a baptism. After the big finale, she wobbles up, a newborn doe. She has to wait until her knees return to normal. They are always pink and indented from the chipping tile floor.

If ever you catch Pip after one of her Long Showers, just look at her knees if you want to learn something you wish you never learned.

The Long Shower was shorter that night. From just beyond the shower door, deep inside Pip's mind, Oona confessed her love just as Pip was leaving for the airport. Oona's hand on the back of Pip's head—her entire hand on Pip's entire head. "I love you," she whispered. Her breath was cool and minty.

Sometimes this narrative took hold of Pip during The Long Shower, but it had nothing to do with lust, or an unrequited yearning for her friend. Pip fell in love with everyone, especially any woman willing to be her friend. These women held her in ways men never did, which was why her sex with them had nothing to do with arousal. The fantasies of sex were fantasies of consummating a standard of love she had earnestly deemed unattainable within tradition.

Pip came silently, her mouth wide open, her face contorted into a shape that looked like the outcome of pain. She had to be quiet because she knew Oona was just down the hall.

After finishing, Pip felt perverted and ashamed, as she typically did. This was similar to when she was a child and used to stick Polly Pockets up her nose during bath time. However, the impact of this perversion and shame settled differently in her adulthood.

The Pollys and Pip had been onto something radical. There was a sense of unknown, no defining motivation. Pip was just pouring body wash on the porcelain and sliding her belly across the tub. Sometimes the soap would sting her vagina. The Pollys would line up for the show, unaware of Pip's forthcoming nostrils.

It was all in good fun until Pip's stepmom, Diana, came calling about her pruney fingers. Then, Pip's neck would compress like an accordion, and she would start lying, all for reasons that eluded her. But immediately after Diana's retreat, Pip would sink right back into the show. She was once ignited by her shame. She ignored the sick twist in her stomach, wrung out by the judgment of adults. She was curious. She kept exploring.

Now, as an adult herself, Pip withered beneath her shame. The twist in her gut was self-sufficient. She couldn't even look back at whatever she had done that made her feel such shame. As soon as it was over, it was like it never happened. Deny, deny, deny. Pip dipped her toe in and blew on the hot spoon, and then hurried away, whispering, "Which toe? What spoon? I did nothing. I saw nothing."

A steady drip fell from the shower door into a sliver of caulk. Pip could hear Oona humming. Her trill vibrated off the marble kitchen counters. Whenever Oona came over, Pip's home was given life. It seemed otherwise uninhabited when it was just Pip; the furniture was washed in gray light, and the air was stale. When Oona was around, the apartment took on a golden breeze.

Wrapped up in the towel, Pip sat on the bathtub, rubbed her knees, and listened to Oona's hum. She wondered when exactly the Pollys had left the picture—when exactly her desires had become so trite (the minty breath, the hand on her head, the "confession of love"). The men in charge, who turn coffee into cocktails and business into pleasure, would pat her knee. "Nice try, woman. Almost. You are longing for love like we want, but your best friend cannot replace the real thing. Call us when you are ready for domestication," they would say.

Pip frowned and tightened her towel around her chest. She could see the grime beneath the shampoo bottles from a distance. She made a mental note to clean the shower before she left, and her face soured at the thought. She preferred cleaning the bathtub, which was never used.

"Pip! Red or white?" Oona yelled from down the hall.

"Whichever!" Pip yelled back. She smiled and checked her knees, then slipped out of the bathroom and into her bedroom. As she dressed, Pip could hear cabinets slamming in the kitchen.

Oona was already making herself at home. She was going to be dog-sitting Geraldine and Chicken while Pip was away, and Pip liked the thought of her best friend using her home. She wondered which mug Oona would choose in the morning, which dining chair she would sit on.

Eight years ago, Pip called Diana,

"There's this girl, Oona. I can't stop looking at her. She's visiting Billy. She's like, I don't know, very cool."

"That's nice. Why don't you ask her to hang out?"

"No! I can't do that. She's too cool. And she's Billy's younger cousin."

"Well, maybe you can ask Billy."

"No, no, Diana. I mean, she's *younger* than me and *already* cooler than me. I'd be so lame if I asked her to hang out."

Billy and Pip met at college, in the summer during their freshman orientation. Billy only spoke to her because he thought she was cute. They became friends when they were placed in the same English course the following fall.

Oona visited during Billy and Pip's second year of college. She was his cousin from Detroit, out east for two weeks to tour schools. She had just started her senior year of high school. On Oona's last night visiting Billy, he and his buddies threw a party. That was where Pip first saw Oona. She was only seventeen and already too mature. She nursed a beer in the corner all night—friendly, but content being on her own.

Years later, Pip and Oona each reached out to Billy separately about being new and friendless in San Francisco. Pip had started a new job as a copy editor for an advertising firm. Oona was getting her M.A. in Urban Planning at San Francisco State.

Billy called Pip, asking if she remembered his cousin, Oona.

"Of course," Pip had squeaked, her throat closing. She remembered how enthralled she had been with the teenage Oona at Billy's party. And although she felt strange to still be so absorbed by the memory of a teenager, Pip let Billy pass her number on to Oona.

One week later, Pip and Oona had coffee. They sat outside in winter, shivering and bewildered by the cold in northern California, but both too polite to suggest going inside.

As Pip sipped her latte and watched Oona's pale, trembling hand pull a strand of hair from her lip gloss, she felt like it was always supposed to unfold in this way. As though cowering at Diana's initial push to reach out was the exact right thing to do. For once, Pip had not suffocated the thing she wanted as soon as she saw it. Now her insides did a little dance.

Soon, coffee turned into dinner, and dinner became movies, and movies became hikes until, one day, Oona suggested they get high and go to the aquarium. Then, there was no need to find a reason to be together. They could just be together.

So, they would walk aimlessly from Lakeshore to Sea Cliff and then back again without saying a word. They would spend Friday evenings lying on the living room floor with their legs dangling up against the walls, scrolling separately on Twitter. A giggle here, a giggle there.

In spending more time with Oona, Pip soon learned that there was nothing factually spectacular about Oona that substantiated her prior awe. Oona was just as alluring and ethereal as ever, but it had nothing to do with anything grandiose. It was her banal behavior that Pip found seductive. It was Oona swallowing. It was Oona sighing. Oona was simple, but she was still such a sight to behold.

The depth of her affect created tiny implosions, like tripping up a step or kicking the heel of the person in front. Everyone wanted to look at Oona, and so everyone tried not to look at her. She was aware of this effect, and she could have taken advantage of it, but instead she handled it with grace and kindness. She never let them know that she could feel the pull of their eyes against her back. When they approached her, she feigned a light surprise, as though she were just becoming conscious of their attention. She wanted them to keep their pride. She wanted them to feel good.

Not only was Oona kind, but she also looked kind. She moved the way women were taught to move; she moved like the women in old movies. Gentle, inviting. When others spoke, Oona tilted her head and listened and nodded and pursed her lips and waited an extra breath before speaking, and then, followed up with a question. Her phone would buzz, and she would toss it away. Her hair was always long. Her legs were always shaved, toned, crossed. Oona embodied every trope of the damsel, and it did not feel like a crime against all women.

For Pip, meeting Oona was such a wonder because of their differences. Pip was not graceful. She was not kind. She inherited judgment from her father, and she held all of this judgment in her shoulders. She was always hunched over, in hiding. Hiding away from others. She did not care about whether anyone felt good.

Oona and Pip were nothing alike. Oona was easy to love, and Pip was not. Pip fell in love with reckless abandon, but Oona did not. Oddly enough, Pip was a lot like her father, while Oona was a lot like Pip's mother (a likeness about which Pip would never know).

Ultimately, all of this contrast made Pip's fantasy of Oona's affection that much more potent. It was impossibility nesting within impossibility—an accumulation of reasons for why something could never be. Reasons spanning time, space, the conscious, and the subconscious. It was despair, desperation, pleasure, and pain infused into something that was nothing and all wrapped up into a secret thing Pip did that would forever remain hidden from Oona.

Sometimes, people bake cakes because they have the resources to do so. It does not mean they understand the value held by each ingredient. It doesn't even mean they have a good reason to bake. A lack of knowledge and good reason does not make the cake any less delicious.

In the living room that evening, Pip and Oona sipped red wine and flipped tarot until they each got the card they wanted. Oona was very good at getting drunk. These nights typically ended with profuse apologies over the state of her inebriation.

"Oh! I'm so so so sorry!"

"For what?"

"I got too drunk. I won't next time! Next time, I won't! Promise."

There was always something childlike about how Oona would beg for Pip's forgiveness. It was in the way Pip was never asking for an apology. It was in the way Oona firmly believed, every time, that she would drink less the next time.

"I'm flawed. I am just flawed," Oona would say, and Pip would nod, hug Oona's head, and marvel—as she always did—at Oona's ability to just "be."

Oona gathered the tarot cards and placed them on the side table. Then, she scooted her butt against Pip's floor to rest her back against the couch.

"How are you feeling?" Oona asked, leaning back.

"Drunk!" Pip giggled. She was lying, belly-up, behind Oona on the couch.

"No, no. About the trip," Oona clarified. She tipped her head back and let it rest against one of Pip's ribs.

Pip drew in a breath.

It was just a work retreat, but there was a surrounding heaviness that Pip had yet to understand. It didn't feel like just a vacation. It felt like something metaphysical and permanent was going to emerge in its wake.

Like she was going to return as a new woman.

Not a better woman, nothing like Oona, but a new one. She was going to have unfollowed her ex-boyfriend on Instagram once and for all or started a successful life coaching business. Or something else. Something redefining.

There was no good reason for this feeling. It was just a thing she heard about—people leaving home for a period of time, being "exposed" to the world, and coming back changed, with a new, special feeling about how small they are, and how small everyone else is, and how nothing matters at all. This worried Pip. It worried her because of Oona. Pip did not want a broader view of the world to make her unrecognizable to Oona, to create an unmanageable distance between the two of them.

In the kitchen later, Oona washed the wine glasses while Pip sorted through the fridge for things that would spoil.

"I have this thing."

Oona nodded for Pip to go on.

"Before I travel, I have to finish every piece of food that might rot. No matter how long the trip is, I need it gone. It's that it has the potential to go bad that bothers me."

"That's not weird," Oona responded. "I can see how that makes sense." She was so good at making others feel like their reality was the right reality.

"Well, there's this half of a red onion I won't get to. No pressure, though," Pip said. "It's not a big deal," she shrugged. In fact, she wanted to beg Oona not to let the onion go to waste, but instead, she doubled down, "It's no big deal."

At the end of the night, Pip handed Oona the key to her home. The exchange felt centuries long. As if, while standing at the entrance, passing the key, all of Pip's old friends got married and had kids, and those kids had kids, and those kids' kids had kids, and the Third World War started destroying everything around them, and the kids' kids' kids had kids, and those kids were troubled with the arduous task of building bomb shelters and learning to fish for the sake of the family lineage, and even then, by this point, the key was only two fingers free from Pip's hand.

Oona hugged Pip twice at the door. If this were one of Pip's fantasies, it would have meant one hug for "goodbye" and another for "I love you. I love you! I love you, and now you have to go before I stop you from going."

On the plane, Pip waited for the lights to dim. While everyone slept, she wept as she often did on planes. Distance was always so stripping and abrasive. It was easier to cry from far away, although she rarely knew what she was crying about.

When Pip landed at her layover in Sydney, her eyes were dry. She thought of the onion, but she didn't know why. By the second flight, she had a lingering feeling that Oona wasn't going to eat it. She knew, then, that it was not that she would return to Oona as someone else or someone unrecognizable, but that she might not return to Oona in the same way. She might have to loosen her grip.

Pip told herself that she would let the onion decide.

For the rest of the work retreat, Pip tried to appreciate the rest of the world. She climbed volcanic mountains and swam next to caged crocodiles. She met strangers who couldn't stop mentioning their lovers. When they asked Pip if she was seeing someone, Pip thought of her best friend, Oona, and she shook her head, 'no.' Then, the strangers would nod over and over again, not knowing what to say. They all had someone guaranteed to finish their produce if and when they needed it. When two people loved each other, that's what they did.

Three weeks later, Pip arrived home in the middle of the night and went straight to the kitchen to see if the onion had been eaten. But she couldn't bring herself to open the refrigerator. Instead, she closed her eyes, pressed her forehead against the refrigerator door, and imagined the inside empty, perhaps even wiped clean with Lysol—no onion in sight.

She imagined that Oona had taken care of the onion, sparing it from rot, just as Pip had asked. She imagined smiling and yelling to the men in charge, "See! Oona will finish my produce! She is enough! There is no such need for the 'real thing.'"

Pip awoke the following morning curled up on the kitchen floor, Geraldine and Chicken licking her ears. The refrigerator door was ajar and beeping. The onion was green.

***

"Babe! Let's go! We're late!" Billy yells from the hall.

This is followed by "Mommy!"

Then "Honey!"

And "Mom!"

What? Pip shrieks. Nobody hears. She stands up from the concrete shower floor. There is a stream of red water circling the drain. The skin on her knee is ripped like rug burn.

Pip dries herself quickly. Her towel hits the floor as she searches the bathroom drawer for a Band-Aid.

"Sissy took my tutu!"

"Have you seen my red sweater?"

"It's not hers; tell her it's mine! It's mine!"

The blood from Pip's knee trickles down her calf and onto the floor. She balls up some toilet paper to stop the flow.

As Pip presses the tissue against her knee, she catches the reflection of herself in the mirror. She is old. But she can tell it is her by the way she stands. Hunching. She tries to straighten up, but the bleeding knee keeps her bent over, stuck in a curve.

In the car later, on the way to their daughters' recital, Billy glances down. At first, Pip thinks he is having a sexual thought, so she pulls her skirt up an inch onto her thigh and waits eagerly for his reaction. Her heart pounds. Billy's brow twitches. These heated moments almost never happen.

Pip can see Billy's face cracking and folding along the lines permanently etched into his skin as he studies her leg. He is old now too. She feels like she is noticing it for the first time. His sandy blonde hair has started to turn white.

He and Oona had always been the only two cousins with blonde. Everyone else in their family was born with hair as dark as night. When Pip married Billy, she remembered looking around at his relatives during their wedding and thinking she looked more like blood than in-law.

Billy clears his throat. He keeps squinting toward Pip's leg, flicking his eyes to and from the road. Pip watches him. When he finally stops in front of a red light, he reaches down and grabs just above her kneecap, and Pip's eyes widen with delight.

"What happened there?" Billy asks.

"Where?"

"There," he says, sticking his finger into the tiny gash on her knee.

"Ow." Pip shoves his pudgy hand away. "I fell. In Zumba," she says.

"Again?" Billy says. His eyes meet Pip's, heavy and intense. Her stomach flips. For a second, she thinks he's learned something he wishes he had never learned.

Joany

Joany still wears bikinis. She has three of them. They are all black. She only wears the black one with the thick ties. Every time her daughters visit, Joany dumps a variety of her possessions onto the bed in the guest room. Often, the pile includes the two unused black bikinis. But her daughters, Liliana and Georgia, do not want their mother's old bikinis. So, Joany's inventory of bikinis has remained the same for the past two decades.

Yesterday, Joany went to the beach wearing the black bikini with the thick ties. As soon as she arrived, she darted head-first into the towering waves. When she dove beneath, she disappeared for a long time. Eventually, her head emerged as a dark speck among the pulpy sea foam. She glistened on the walk back to her towel.

JOANY

She's always belonged to the ocean.

When Joany goes to the beach, the other Montauk ladies pretend not to see her, but they are always eyeing their husbands, who watch her from their periphery. They don't understand why she chooses not to live with the extravagance that they do, why she avoids their luncheons and cocktail hours, why she always rents and never buys. Those mean, women-policing women were never suited for her. They are too content to monopolize an already colonized land, but Joany is resistant to "settling" as they have. She does not want to play bridge at the country club on Tuesday afternoons. She does not want to become stuck in, or to, a single place in order to feel whole.

Today is the day after her fifty-ninth birthday, and Joany is on the verge. She is not copacetic, and she has not been for a while. She could cry again, but instead Joany stares at her husband while she eats lunch (a handful of almonds and a non-fat Greek yogurt).

Her husband is sitting in the office obsessing over Canada, climate change, his new truck, and the "next generation," whom he will never meet, because he is slowly, slowly dying. She loves him still, but they are becoming more like roommates, their conversations blunted by financial decisions and the allocation of household tasks.

I guess we're doing this thing, Joany thinks. She is referring to the end of life.

Joany can't peel her eyes away from him. His posture irks her. "Sit up," she mumbles. "Sit up," she repeats, straightening up herself. *Look at him. His pale, naked back—those seven widely spaced, protruding hairs are longer than the hair on his head!* she thinks.

Joany wiggles in her seat. They have been in the Hamptons too long. She is ready to move again. She wants to visit Liliana, in San Diego, next.

Liliana is the good daughter. Obliging, thoughtful. Almost perfect. She is attentive to the condition of the family unit (but only from afar). She can tap the doorknob to check for fire on the other side; she'll never open the door.

Joany's husband doesn't like San Diego. He won't go with her to see their daughter. He does his own thing. After the Hamptons, he wants to shoot guns on his newly acquired Canadian land.

So, Joany and her husband will go their separate ways for a wink, escaping one another until they remember that it is not the other they wish to escape but themselves instead. Then, they'll come together again, and stare at each other, and talk about chores and finances. This cycle will repeat until they die.

Joany and her husband are all each other have now. This strikes Joany from time to time. Technically, she still has Liliana and Georgia, but they are both in college. And even though Georgia is only twenty minutes north of the city, it feels as though she is farther away than Liliana. Georgia forgot to call yesterday. She is the less-good daughter. Saccharine when it serves her. She is not the one who will be caring for them in old age.

JOANY

Joany can hear her phone buzzing in the other room.

There she is. A day late, Joany smirks to herself.

She lets the call go to voicemail and reaches across the table, pulling over a list she wrote yesterday on a bar napkin while waiting for her husband. He was late to her birthday dinner, stuck in a game of online poker.

The list reads:

Goat/brie

Yogurt

Dr. Rhemal eczema cream

Water shoes for Georgia – Amazon

~~Patrón Patrón~~

San Pellegrino

Coffee

For so many years, Joany excelled at lists like these. It's unclear when exactly this competence took hold. Somehow, the muscle was always there. It was just a matter of when to flex.

Joany tosses the last almond into her mouth and opens her laptop. She goes to Amazon and orders a pair of water shoes for Georgia's study abroad trip to Rome. She can hear her phone buzzing again in the other room. When it stops, a text message pings on Joany's computer screen.

Georgia: *Mom! Call me back.*

Joany confirms the Amazon order and closes her laptop. She glances at her empty yogurt cup—her last one, according to the list. She'll have to go to the store soon.

Joany wiggles again. Wifehood, motherhood, then wifehood again. This kept her tied to her lists for long enough.

In the other room, Joany's husband clears his throat repeatedly. Joany waits for him to stop. The way he hacks with such little self-awareness is impressive. He is just like most men. They are always coughing something up and spitting it out, their bodies overcompensating for the thoughts in their heads.

Is this really it? My lists and his phlegm, and then we die? Joany thinks.

She imagines selling it all before they go, getting rid of every belonging, leaving just a pile of lists coated in phlegm—one piece of paper stuck to another by a glob of her husband's saliva.

Joany's husband continues to hack. Her phone buzzes again from the other room. She rises to her feet but remains standing in one place.

The hacking, the buzzing, the hacking, the buzzing.

Joany can't discern whether it was always like this or if she is just now gaining consciousness in the second half of life.

Next, a vibration below distracts her—her stomach. Growling because she is still trying to lose weight (she is always trying to lose weight).

Now it's the hacking, the buzzing, the growling. The hacking, the buzzing, the growling.

This must be purgatory, Joany thinks.

But it is really just womanhood. She did it all by herself, to herself, with just one knife.

She's only now contemplating the knife—held up against her the whole time. Only now lowering it from her neck.

While she is unperturbed to see the knife in her own hand, she is thrown off by the hand itself. The hand is not her hand. The hand belongs to her mother. Did all the mothers that came before lower a knife to find their mother's hand?

"Hey, Kookie, is that my phone or yours?" her husband yells.

"Mine," Joany peeps.

"Who is it?"

"Georgia. She wants to wish me a happy birthday."

"Aren't you going to answer it?" he asks, irritated.

"Sorry. I didn't realize you could hear the buzz over your own bark," she snips.

"Huhmff?" is all he says, unaware he was making any noise at all.

Joany wanders into the bedroom. Her phone continues to buzz. The shades are still drawn, and the bed is unmade. She could crawl back in. No one would question her. No one would need her. There was a time when everyone needed her all the time. She would have killed to crawl back into bed. But this bed is a different bed to her now. It isn't as inviting as it once was.

Joany grabs her phone from the nightstand just as the call ends. She goes to Georgia's contact and dials her back immediately, but Georgia doesn't answer right away. The dial tone persists until what feels like the last possible ring. Joany watches dust particles float around a beam of light. Eventually, the tone cuts. There is a long silence on the other end.

"Hello?" Joany says.

"Hey, sorry, I'm sending a text. One sec."

Joany waits.

"Hey," Georgia repeats.

"Hi, Honey. How's it going? Just calling you back," Joany waits again. She is suddenly tired. Maybe she will try a nap after the belated birthday call. "Hellooo?" Joany sings.

"Yeah, thanks, sorry. How are you?" Georgia blurts. "I was just checking to see if you ordered those water shoes for Italy yet," she asks.

Joany is silent. Not surprised, but hurt nonetheless, and a little angry even, that she did, in fact, order the shoes.

"Mom?" Georgia says.

Joany considers canceling the order and making Georgia buy them herself. But what if Georgia forgets? What if she goes swimming in a river with a strong current? What if she slips and cracks her head open on a rock? What if she drowns? All because Joany canceled the order.

Joany tilts back onto the unmade bed. She loosens the grip on her cell phone, letting it rest against her neck.

Through the receiver, Joany can hear Georgia, "Mom. Mom! Hello? Did I lose you?" In the other room, her husband starts hacking again.

Joany presses two fingers into her temples. Her stomach groans. She rubs her forehead, trying to mentally sever her hand from the rest of her body, so that it would feel as though someone else was giving her a massage.

Perhaps it's not so bad that the knife is still there. Maybe she can use it to cut off her hand.

Willie

There are no more small, precious things. Willie's relationship with Liam was the very last one. But that came and went. Everyone missed it because it became obscured by rumor, mistaken for something big and impure instead. The real truth was that the sexual nature of Willie's relation to Liam was never really sexual. Willie had sex with Pei, and Pei came first.

Willie met Pei in the '90s in the Vons parking lot off of Olympic. Pei was new to the area and living out of his car. He had been twenty minutes into scraping pigeon shit from his windshield when Willie rushed by on foot, out of toilet paper and lacking the same luxury as the pigeons. Willie was dressed in a leopard robe, pink cowboy boots, and a yellow chunky sweater. The sweater was unraveling due to overuse. It was a gift, stitched by his late grandmother, who used to kiss him on the forehead and whisper in his ear about love, reassuring him that his love was just as good as all other love.

Willie noticed Pei as he scurried past—clearly a newcomer, as nobody parked in the leftmost corner of the lot—but Pei didn't notice Willie. When Willie emerged a little while later, four-pack of two-ply wedged in his armpit, he wandered over to Pei's car and offered a nod of approval at the nearly clear windshield.

"Town hall must've run long today," Willie joked. He was referring to the congregation of pigeons perched on the Vons sign above them. Pei was unamused, and Willie shrugged and continued out of the parking lot.

Six weeks later, by happenstance, Pei moved into Willie's apartment complex. Neither of them remembered the pigeon interaction until a year and a half into dating when the Vons was being torn down, replaced by a Whole Foods (which was later replaced by a Planet Fitness), and Pei remarked on "that horrible summer spent smelling like boiling pigeon shit."

When they started dating, they kept their separate apartments. Even many years in, Pei refused to let go of his place. The years he spent in his car made him possessive of his own space. Willie always wished Pei would move in with him, but he never said a word. It wasn't until decades later when Willie grew sick, that Pei finally moved in to care for him.

Pei's move in with Willie marked the start of a continuous flow of new tenants in and out of his former place. It began with two twenty-something UCLA sorority girls and their cosigning parents, who took over the place with a feverish enthusiasm. In a single day, the moms brought in pink fairy lights and miniature cacti, while the dads nailed a Ring camera to the door, and the girls spent the day at Ikea, returning later with a floor mirror and a doormat. The doormat displayed the silhouette of a black cat directly below the words, "Welcome to the Pussy Pad." The girls' parents visited often, dropping off "care packages" with next month's rent and utilities, and one of the dads always had something to say about the doormat.

Before the arrival of the Pussy Pad, the apartment complex had been exclusively occupied by older gay men, brought in by friends of friends of friends—a comfortable place during a tumultuous era. The Pussy Pad and its inhabitants were a new development, defining a rise in rent prices, "shifts in the discourse," the transcendence from overt into covert forms of discrimination.

The girls and their parents only ever knew Pei and Willie after Willie got sick. They were always smiling sympathetically, offering "thoughts and prayers" whenever they saw Pei, whom they assumed was Willie's nurse. Not once did they formally introduce themselves—if such neighborly courtesies were the way of the world when Pei had moved into the complex, there would have been no Willie and Pei. To be a neighbor in America was beginning to mean something else. Nobody said hello anymore.

Except for Liam. Liam was an exception.

Liam grew up next door to Willie and Pei. He and his parents moved in around a decade ago, during the recession, when PBS laid off two-thirds of its employees, and they had to sell the house and start anew. Liam was in the middle of his first year of high school and sour over transferring schools.

"Like my New York days," Liam's father grinned with unconvincing positivity as he and Liam unpacked the U-Haul, loading boxes into the ground-floor apartment. His father was always looking for silver linings, which garnered little response within a trio that spent holidays watching movies in lieu of making conversation. It was always a pleasant time. Nothing real was ever discussed. They were all a lot alike, and yet, they didn't know anything about each other.

Liam's mother was an anxious little woman, but she was talkative and kind. His father was introverted and value-driven. And Liam was a combination of the two: anxious and introverted and kind. However, there was a lightness to both of his parents that Liam did not inherit. Neither of them quite knew how to deal with this.

As Liam grew into himself, he started keeping his shades drawn and his bedroom door closed. He started hiding away, as if to anticipate total and irreversible destruction out in the real world. Liam was discovering solace in the blackened corners of his room, where no one, not even he, could witness evidence of a lingering pain that gnawed at him as he came of age.

The pain was like a hole, originating in his stomach, that stretched wider every year. It swallowed up pieces of Liam from inside out. Anyone trying to know him was quickly stunted by the hole, which siphoned Liam off from himself long before they could get to him.

This gave Liam a certain affectation in public. It was as if there was always something scaring him. It made everyone fall in love with him. Which made Liam want to run. But they were not really in love with Liam; they were motivated by novelty. They did not have a hole like him, but they wanted to know what it was like. Looking at them reminded Liam of his hole. And so, often, he ran.

Willie always lived next door to Liam. He smoked out on his porch many times a day, and so he caught glimpses of Liam running from time to time. Unlike the girls who were drawn in by novelty, Willie's curiosity toward Liam was piqued by recognition. However, it was unclear why Liam seemed so familiar until the Summer of 2014.

In the Summer of 2014, Willie's mother passed away. So, he returned home to North Carolina to cremate her and deal with her estate. While Willie sorted through his mother's belongings, he stumbled across an old photo book—fading images of him as an infant into his teenage years. There was one particular photograph of him as a teenager, holding a fish as big as his forearm, smiling and frowning simultaneously. It was the same pain, the same affectation. Right there, in that squiggle smile, was the source of his affinity for Liam. Willie's laugh had echoed through his dead mother's home that afternoon as he clapped the photo book closed.

There is no escaping the self. Even after moving away, remaking a life, and discarding all remnants of childhood, there was no escape from the self.

After emptying his mother's home entirely into a dumpster, Willie returned to Los Angeles with an invigorating new fascination. It was born out of a subtle meditation on whether Liam would crack and free himself from the prison of his own defensive creation instead of hardening like concrete, just as Willie did with age. Watching out for this was like peeking through the airplane seats at the kicking child in the row behind. One can glare at it, but best just to lean forward until the plane lands. This was the strategy Willie adopted as he watched Liam grow up.

And so, long before the Pussy Pad occupied the communal front porch, Willie would sit out there, hand rolling cigarettes, watching Liam drag his feet to and from school, soccer practice, guitar lessons, and friends' houses, growing awkwardly tall and dying his hair green, and slowly developing a sense of entrenched contentment, impervious to any true feeling. The hole just kept getting bigger. It pained Willie, but there was nothing to be done except let Liam go.

Occasionally, Willie was unable to help himself. He'd call out to Liam—odd remarks, commenting on his clothing, or the size of his instrument, or the girl that crept out of his bedroom window the night prior. Willie just wanted to see Liam smile, to get a sense of whether or not, and to what extent, the hole had yet to damage him.

So, Willie would comment something marginally flirtatious, all fun and games, nothing really serious, and Liam would stop, smile politely, maybe even chuckle, proving he was raised right even if not exceptionally well.

One time, when Liam was going through an "overalls phase," Willie yelled from across the lawn, "D'you know boys in my time used to wear those without shirts underneath!"

Liam had laughed in a breathy way. Willie never once thought his teasing made Liam uncomfortable. If Pei were around, he'd swat Willie on the arm, and Willie would shrug. It seemed like flirting, but it wasn't. It was poking. It was watching. It was a form of caring. Willie knew this. Pei knew this. On some level, Liam knew this too.

Liam's father, however, was not fond of Willie's comments. Liam's parents would often bicker about Willie, about whether or not to confront him. This resulted in a callousness from Liam's parents, interpreted by Pei as homophobia. Despite Liam's attempts to reassure his parents of Willie's innocence and Willie's efforts to quell Pei's assumptions about Liam's parents, this playful rapport between Liam and Willie became clouded by the tension between Pei and Liam's father. Eventually, since Liam never felt compelled to complain, his parents let it be (for the most part).

There was only one time when Liam's father confronted Willie. Liam was helping his mother repot the plants on their front porch. The sun was high in the sky. They were halfway through an exceptionally hot and humid summer. Liam had managed to keep himself locked away in the air-conditioning for most of the day, but his mother had had enough and dragged him out for fresh air. Willie was sitting next door, out on his porch, smoking a cigarette, waiting for the doctor to call, unaware he would soon learn he was dying.

As Willie's cigarette smoke wafted over from his porch, Liam's mother kept coughing louder than necessary. This made Liam uncomfortable. He didn't want her to make a scene. He cleared his throat, and she raised an eyebrow. One of the bigger fights Liam ever had with his mother. Eventually, she acquiesced, channeling her agitation into the soil. They worked quietly and efficiently, ignoring Willie's stares.

At some point, Liam worked up a sweat rearranging the newly potted plants, so he slid his shirt off. When Willie noticed, his face lit up. Liam's mother was the only reason for his hesitation. Willie took a moment, stroking his forearm, watching, thinking. His head waddled as he weighed certain consequences. Then, eventually, a whistle escaped Willie's mouth.

This put an abrupt halt to Liam's mother's gardening.

As she shifted her weight from one foot to the other, anxiously reconciling with what to do about the middle-aged man who had just whistled at her teenage son, Willie felt his blood flutter. Her refusal to look his way made him giddy.

Willie leaned forward in his chair, placing an elbow on his crossed leg and his head in his palm. He waited eagerly. He could see her neck fading into a crimson red. Liam looked over at his mother but continued to pour dirt into a pot as if nothing had happened, hoping she would rejoin him.

Instead, she disappeared inside.

"Uh-oh," Willie said with a smile on his face. "She's upset it wasn't for her."

Liam chuckled and then immediately fell silent, his own amusement a surprise to himself. He kept working for a moment. Then, he peered toward his apartment to see if anyone was nearby, turned to Willie and whispered, "C'mon, you can't do that shit in front of my parents, man."

Willie smirked and started rolling himself another cigarette.

Liam took a break, finding a seat on the porch steps. As he watched a crow peck at a loaf of bread in the street, the implication of his prior statement dawned on him—that in the absence of his parents, this kind of flirtation was allowed.

Willie lit his second cigarette while Liam's mind began to wander, wondering.

Wondering whether he might actually like Willie's comments, whether he liked Willie or would take to another man's attention for that matter. A small part of him liked the attention. Was the removal of his shirt a subconscious desire for Willie's gaze? Or was it just ego?

Now, Liam's long-standing attraction to women was on trial, which didn't necessarily worry him as much as it knocked his understanding of a common truth.

It was like the color red was being redefined as blue. In the long run, it didn't matter if red was blue and blue was now red, but in the immediate short term, it would be a remarkable new reality to grasp.

Liam committed to comparing "blue" and "red" for a little while. He thought about a man, a naked man, then a woman, a naked woman. But one naked woman quickly turned into three naked women. Then, three naked women became a bed full of naked women, holding one another, biting into soft stone fruits, juice dripping down their necks and onto their breasts.

It appeared red was to remain red, and blue was to remain blue, but now suddenly Liam had aroused himself, and he was unintentionally angled in Willie's direction. He couldn't get up and risk exposing himself further, so he stayed put, bent over, unmoving. Even worse, Liam could hear his father's footsteps approaching from inside the apartment.

In a feeble attempt to hide his erection, Liam lunged for his shirt, trying to pull it down past his hips. But this was ineffective. When Liam's father emerged, he took one look at his son's penis, then one look at Willie, and his eyes bulged from their sockets.

"Seventeen! He's seventeen!" Liam's father shoved Liam inside.

THERE IS NO ESCAPE

"Excuse me?" Willie flicked his cigarette, the ash dispersing in a gust of wind. He should have been offended by the implied accusation, but his eyes were bright. He was smiling like a child caught coloring on the walls.

Willie held his tongue as Liam's father continued to yell. It was the loudest Willie—and the neighborhood—had ever heard him yell. Willie wondered if Liam was standing close enough inside to see it all; if his father's first real display of negativity would transfer somehow—model for Liam how to grant himself the same allowances. Liam's father yelled for two minutes straight without taking one breath, and Willie's grin did not falter once.

Later that day, Willie received the call confirming that the mole behind his right eye was cancerous, and even then, Willie did not stop grinning. He was imagining the hole in Liam's stomach after hearing his father yell. The hole that held hostage every feeling Liam ever had. He was imagining it shrinking away into nothing.

For a long time after that incident, Liam assumed that Willie's extended retreat from his own porch was due to his father. He felt guilty for causing the implosion. He considered writing Willie a note, apologizing on behalf of his father. But then days, weeks, months went by, and Liam got distracted by things like Algebra II and Lily P's pool party. As the distance from the event grew, Liam's consideration for Willie dwindled until one day he didn't care.

After Liam graduated high school, he stuck around for a couple more years. He noticed Willie getting sick.

Sometimes, if Willie were wrapped up in blankets out on his porch, Liam would wave from a distance.

Eventually, Liam saved enough money to move out of his parents' place. Shortly after he moved out, Willie died. Pei was at his side, half a chunky sweater in hand. He had just taken up knitting. On the same day Willie was buried, the Pussy Pad moved to New York City.

Now, Pei's former apartment lies vacant, littered with spider webs. Occasionally, he will spot a leasing agent unlocking the front door, a small group of young people perched on their tiptoes behind him. The rent prices have risen once again. The apartment is charming, but no one will commit. They all think they can do better.

Pei spends most mornings on the porch, where Willie used to sit. He is still teaching himself how to knit, but he is an impatient student. He has yet to learn how to correct his mistakes, so when he messes up, he tosses the entire thing in the trash, knitting needles and all. Sometimes, Liam's parents see the disposed yarn overflowing in the small dumpster behind their units, and they wonder who would waste such good yarn.

Felix & Emma

When Felix's driver opens the door to the black Cadillac, Felix shines a gummy grin up at Emma. He is half-blind; he has purple skin and pins for ankles. Sometimes, it is hard to remember that he is still human.

Felix uses his arms to lift his legs out of the vehicle as his driver retrieves the walker. Emma offers her hand, but Felix scowls and waves her away, rocking up and onto the walker by himself. The efficiency of his rejection is unsettling but not unfamiliar.

"You look good, darling," Felix grumbles, heading for the automatic sliding doors.

Emma hurries after him. "Nice to see you, Oscar!" she shouts over her shoulder at the driver, but Oscar is already pulling away from the curb.

At the entrance to the building, Emma stops for a moment. She watches a cloud of vapor roll out of Oscar's window. His blinker is off as he attempts an illegal left turn onto Jackson Avenue. She waits until Oscar pulls safely into the street and out of view. A car accident would be inconvenient. They need him later to return Felix to the nursing home after the appointment.

In the lobby, Emma just barely beats Felix to the elevators. She clicks the button on his behalf, bouncing and tossing her arm in the air, pleased with herself. Then, she pulls out the details of the appointment as they wait for the elevator to arrive.

"We're headed to the second floor. Two-nineteen, I think. Let me just double-check. Yes. Two-nineteen," she says.

Felix nods, his breath heavy—a useful reminder for Emma to breathe, as she so often holds her breath in public.

"Have you had a nice morning?" Emma asks.

"No," he replies.

"Oh, sorry," Emma says. Her voice devours itself. She imagines Felix, alone, in a room, the television playing local news at a low level, his daily dose of interaction when the nurse pops in to shove blood thinners down his throat.

"What about you?" Felix asks.

The elevator dings, and the doors part.

"Yeah, I had a fine morning. Thanks," Emma lies. She extends an arm, holding the elevator open for Felix to pass through even though the sensors on the doors are in working condition. Her arm does more to get in the way than provide any real sense of safety.

Once in the elevator, Emma studies the digital display at the top as it shifts from "L" to "1" to "2." When the doors part on "2," she throws another awkward arm out for Felix to pass.

Felix's walker brushes Emma's knuckles as he exits the elevator.

Emma recoils in self-ridicule.

These gestures, this dance! Attempts to justify her use. They only emphasize the cosmetic nature of her aid. She could disappear, and Felix wouldn't know the difference. He is not ready to relinquish all autonomy. His daughters would scoff, and roll their eyes, and rub their faces if they knew this was where their one-hundred-and-fifty plus mileage reimbursement went every Tuesday afternoon.

"Take a seat right here. I'll check you in," Emma points to the closest waiting room chair and heads for reception. "Felix Orlov for Dr. Peña? It should be a three o'clock appointment," she says. She feels like she is imitating a grown-up.

"Yes," the receptionist bares her teeth, attempting a smile. There is lipstick on her left incisor. "I just need you to verify his birthday," she says. Her eyelids are at half mast, weighed down by lengthy eyelash extensions.

A flash of worry crosses Emma's face. "Oh," she says. "I've never had to give his birthday before." Emma glances back at Felix, who is watching the television positioned in the top right corner of the room. "Am I allowed to ask him?" Emma stutters.

"It isn't a test," the receptionist replies.

"Right," Emma laughs weakly. Her head drops. She turns to Felix.

"Three, seventeen, nineteen-thirty-one," he interjects, his eyes still glued to the television.

"Got it," the receptionist chirps.

Emma hesitates, stunted (this dance!). It's as if she has walked onto the stage in the middle of a rehearsal—a stage manager contracted to make things better, but now the actors have their own agenda.

Emma surrenders onto the seat next to Felix. As they wait for Felix's name to be called, she pretends to watch a fly buzz around the room. Eventually, her phone vibrates—a text from Felix's oldest daughter, Carol, checking in on the appointment. The text reminds Emma of a photograph from his other daughter that she's meant to share with Felix.

Emma scrolls to find a photograph of Felix's youngest daughter, Lauren, sitting next to three poodles. She shows Felix the screen, and he breaks into a smile. "Lauren wanted me to show you this," she says.

Felix reaches for the phone. He looks longingly at the picture.

This confuses Emma. She remembers Lauren making a snide remark at some point during her onboarding—something about it being good Emma was "irrelevant" (meaning not family and not anyone he knows personally). Apparently, Felix is nicer to strangers than family.

Now, Felix's affection toward the photograph seems inconsistent. Emma wonders if Lauren had lied to her for some reason about Felix's distaste for his own family. For a moment, she feels bad for the poor old man.

But then Felix says, "I used to have five dogs. Back in Chicago," and it's clear he's lit up by the dogs and not his daughter.

Felix's eyes glaze over as his mind trails the memory of his beloved dogs. "I had to give them up when I came out here," he explains. "I want to get another one. Maybe two."

Emma lets out a small sigh. She is oddly relieved that the validity of Lauren's statement is preserved. It makes Felix's current existence less sad.

"Where you stay now, do they not allow dogs?" Emma asks. She avoids the term "nursing home" because she is afraid it will remind him he is elderly.

"Oh no, they do. It's just—"

"Well, yeah, dogs are a lot of work. Too much work," Emma interrupts. Felix is unresponsive, and Emma shrinks away, worried she may have sounded patronizing. "I mean, that would be too much work for me even," she adds, shrinking deeper into her seat. She imagines shrinking and shrinking until she is just a mouth in a chair, so far-removed Felix would have to embrace the notion that such a terrible interaction could only be due to the fact that he chose to converse with a chair.

Emma glances self-consciously at the nurses behind reception. She knows they are listening. She wonders what they think. Probably that Felix deserves better than her. Better than a girl like her. Older than twenty-four. Someone with a bed frame rather than a mattress on the floor. Someone who would know how to speak to him, how to avoid a tone of voice that suggests he is mentally disadvantaged, how to utter the term "nursing home" without it sounding like an insult.

This is a man who used to cut deals with the Russian mob, according to a text accidentally sent to her from Lauren last weekend. *Finally watched Godfather movie with Jimmy. Pacino nothing like Dad. Maybe Italian different from Russian. Idk! Overall, eh. 2/10.* Lauren meant to send it to Carol.

Maybe Felix's mob experience means he could handle the physicality of owning a couple of dogs at age ninety-two. Maybe Emma is wrong to assume his body would fail him. She does not know about the daily lives of dogs. In seventh grade, when so many of Emma's friends started getting puppies, Emma told them her father was allergic. Really, he just didn't want to raise a "spoiled bitch."

A puppy was the last thing Emma ever asked her father for. She learned to stop wanting. Now, in her young adulthood, Emma's curiosity has waned as she leans into the warm, well-understood areas of inaction. She sits in the comfort of "I don't know. It's too difficult" instead of excavating the ways in which her father dissuaded her from the many curiosities of life.

Emma looks over at Felix for any evidence that she may have offended him. But Felix just breathes, unaffected. He zooms in on the picture of his daughter and the poodles, a smile stretching across his face. He tries repeatedly to zoom in on just the poodles, but the phone screen bounces back, unable to zoom in any further (unable to cut Lauren out). No photograph has ever made Emma smile like this. As she watches Felix, something sharp punctures her stomach. Then her chest tightens, and her breath catches deep within her sternum, as though weights tied to her ankles were dragging her under water.

"Felix?" a nurse calls.

"Oh," Emma pops up, her face flushed. "Looks like they're ready for us." She offers Felix her hand. It shakes in the wake of the almost-panic attack. Felix doesn't notice. He ignores her help once again, using the armrests of his chair instead.

"The doctor will be in shortly," the nurse says as the three of them shuffle toward the examination room.

"How long is shortly?" Felix snips. A common phrase of his.

The nurse is unamused. She forces a laugh and shuts the door.

Once alone in the room together, Felix trips, trying to get onto the chair. The footrest below knocks into his ankles because he lacks the mobility to lift his foot off the ground. Emma is too naive to know that she can just prop the footrest vertically to move it out of his way. As she stutters and grunts, trying to keep Felix from hitting the floor, a nurse rushes in to assist them. She lifts the footrest and lowers Felix gently onto the chair, glaring at Emma on her way out. Emma drops her gaze, contrite, and takes a seat on a small stool in the corner.

As the doctor's voice echoes from the adjacent room, Emma watches Felix nod in and out of sleep. A vent blows frigid, sterile air against the back of her neck. She shivers. Next door, the doctor exits the other room. The door slams behind him. Emma waits, watching the door. His footsteps are soft, then loud, and then soft again. When the doctor does not arrive, she glances back at Felix.

His eyes are open now. He is looking at Emma. The slam must have woken him.

Emma grins. "What about a fish instead of a dog? A friend of mine just bought a fish," she offers.

Felix shrugs. "What kind of fish?" he asks.

"She got a betta fish. They're beautiful. Fighter fish. Apparently, they have to be alone in their tanks. Otherwise, they'll kill the others," Emma raises her eyebrows.

Felix likes this. He nods repeatedly, losing himself in thought. Perhaps he is imagining a betta fish tearing a goldfish to shreds. "What would you name your betta fish?" he asks.

Emma shakes her head. "I don't know. What are typical fish names anyway?" she says. Felix purses his lips, uncertain. "If you got a dog, what would you name it?" Emma asks.

Felix hesitates, drifting away for a moment. His expression makes Emma want to take back the question. Eventually he says, "Anna."

"Anna," Emma repeats. It's not the name she expected. It's a human name. "Pretty," she chokes. Maybe Felix didn't hate every single person close to him.

Felix shifts in his seat.

"Are you, um. . ."

Emma sits up, attentive.

"Are you going to be in here for the appointment?" he asks.

"Oh. I thought so, but I don't have to be." Felix nods, cutting her off. "Sure!" Emma shoots up, "Of course! Sorry."

"It's just a private matter."

"Of course, no, of course." Emma heads for the door. "I'll be just waiting out there if you need anything." Emma opens the door to find the doctor standing on the other side. "Sorry," she startles, shifting out of his way. "I'll be right out there if he needs anything. Just yell for me," she repeats to the doctor.

He gives a curt nod. "How are we doing, Felix?" he says, entering the room.

"We? Well, I can't say how you're doing," Felix bites back. Another common phrase of his.

The doctor chortles and shuts the door firmly behind him, leaving Emma standing alone in the hall.

"I'm just going to be right here. If he needs anything," Emma repeats again, this time to the receptionist with the lipstick on her tooth. She glances up at Emma with a blank expression.

Over the next hour, Emma sits patiently in the waiting room. Occasionally, she hears the doctor's voice boom from down the hall. Felix does not emerge for a while. She waits, crossing and uncrossing her legs, scrolling through her phone, biting her cuticles, staring up at the television (a forest fire destroys celebrity homes). She watches various patients exit with their middle-aged kids or professionally trained caretakers. One son of an elderly woman with bandages over both eyes can't get enough of Emma's freezing, erect nipples as he guides his mother out of the office.

"Andrew?" she yells when her cane hits the front door. He stammers, flummoxed, peeling away from Emma's breasts to help his ailing mother.

Emma was going to be a dancer. She had the drive, the diligence, and the overbearing parent. She possessed the ideal amount of masochism too; her suffering over perfection was impressive, as was her dedication to starvation. From the age of four and for two consecutive decades, Emma worked until there was nothing left of herself. When she eventually landed a spot with the Alvin Ailey American Dance Theatre, she was surprised to find that what she thought she always wanted didn't feel as good as she thought it would when she got it. The day after her acceptance, she resigned and never again felt the urge to dance.

In the absence of dance, Emma soon discovered that she didn't have much of an identity or personality. So, she moved to Miami, where she found others dealing with a similar predicament. Emma rents a room in a fraternity house near Miami University. She found Felix on Craigslist. He covers the cost of the room.

Now, she tells herself he's a temporary job as she considers going back to school for something normal, like accounting. But she doesn't really want to be an accountant. Nor does she want to be a therapist, or a businessman, or a teacher, or a salesperson. Emma's search for the future of her life has proven challenging. She doesn't know how to desire her own becoming. She's never had to want to become. She's only ever been told what she wants to become. Emma never misses dance, but often now, she pines for the sense of meaning it gave her.

"Emma?" Felix calls from the hall.

A thin string of saliva extends from Emma's mouth as she rips away her left thumb cuticle.

"Coming!" she shouts.

Felix is already out of the examination room and waddling down the hall. He has a bandage over his right eye but is otherwise able to navigate with his left.

"You alright? Everything alright?" Emma asks as they head out of the office.

"Fine," Felix exhales.

"Good. Here, let me call Oscar and make sure he's downstairs."

On the way down, Emma repeats her earlier dance—pressing buttons and holding open elevator doors. They make it safely to the curb, where Oscar waits, waving away vaporized air.

"He thinks I don't know what he's smoking," Felix whispers bitterly to Emma as they approach the Cadillac.

At the curb, Felix helps himself into the Cadillac, while Oscar takes his walker and places it in the trunk. Emma stands nearby, looking for something to do.

"Do you want me to buckle you in?" she nearly pleads.

Felix just shakes his head 'no.' He shifts to the side and pulls out a small wad of bills. He thumbs through the ones before pulling out a five and handing it to Emma.

"You're a good girl," Felix says, shoving the money into Emma's palm.

"Thanks," Emma almost laughs, taken aback by such a dated gesture.

"Buy yourself something nice. Anything you want," Felix says.

"I don't know what I'll get," Emma responds. She tries to think of what item a five might buy her. A pack of gum, nail polish remover, maybe.

"Whatever you want!" Felix waves his hand in the air, quickly irritated by Emma's indecision.

"Okay. Sorry. I will." Emma folds up the five and places it into her pocket before he can take it back. "Thank you," she says.

Felix nods, leaning away from Emma, his legs scrunching together. His eyes are cast down. Emma wonders if he's drifting into sleep again. She tilts in, trying to get a sense of what exactly is going on. She doesn't realize he is waiting for something. When whatever he is waiting for does not come, Felix looks up at Emma, increasingly more irritated.

"Uh, it was nice to see you, Felix. I'll see you again soon, yeah?"

Felix nods again, still waiting. Emma squints and shakes her head, trying to figure out what is going on. Oscar shuts the trunk and gets into the driver's seat. He pulls his door closed and starts the car.

Then, suddenly, it dawns on her. Felix is going to let Emma shut his door.

Me and You (and Everyone Else)

I want everything, everywhere, always, to be forever. Nobody is allowed to leave me. Everything is to stay exactly as it is. That way, I'll always be smiling because I'll always be happy. Happy to know nothing better and nothing worse. Happy to expect nothing more. Happy to settle with the mediocrities of me and you and everyone else.

But just because Millie, Ricky, and I took our clothes off, and just because we all touched everything, and just because we all did everything, and just because everything was equal, doesn't then mean that we are all best friends forever and ever. Millie and Ricky might stay friends for a bit because they say they love each other, but it won't be for forever. Nothing, nowhere, ever is forever.

The idea of forever is only within reach under delusion. Someone with an advanced degree can write a paper that suggests forever, and that paper can be signed by those in search of forever, but still, this is no sure thing. The people at the 24-Hour Fitness make it seem like we are locked in for life, but then they tell us that if we fall ill or break a bone we can leave without any further financial commitment. If we want out of forever all we have to do is break our own arms.

Today, I woke up without a shirt on and the vague recollection of tossing the sweaty garment onto the bathroom floor in the middle of the night. This is the first summer in five years that I am lucid. It's more out of laziness than any genuine effort to be good. It's showing me how much time there is in a day, in an hour—in a minute! Now, I fixate on ways to spend it, ways to avoid its influence.

If I walk to the grocery store rather than drive, I'll spend an hour total—thirty minutes there, thirty minutes back. If I write an email by hand first and then again on the computer, it will take twice as long. If I throw away the flowers on the dining room table before they start to smell, I can go out and buy new ones—that's nearly half the day gone if I go during rush hour. As long as I spend time, I'll never have to worry about wasting it. I envy those who obsess over saving time, rather than spending or wasting, but those people are either disgustingly happy or otherwise raising children.

Saving, spending, not wasting—no matter the route, these are all just subversions from the moments when time starts to act on us. We are consumed with acting on time the way we so effortlessly did when we were young. Spending time spending time just to spend time or saving time to save time just to save time. Everything is boiling down to snapshots between and around each other—one spends time while the other saves, the two of them wanting something from time but nothing to do with each other.

If everything was everything for forever, time would not carry this much weight. Things would be slightly different for me. I would be one of those girls who posts dozens of pictures of herself, making the same blasé expression in the same boring, ugly-ironic outfit. Then, at the end of my life, I'd be content, left with hundreds of pictures of myself making the same face and wearing the same clothes. More fulfilling ways to spend the time would have never crossed my mind. Unfortunately, forever is a curious thing and I am not one of those girls. So instead, time eats me alive if I don't find something to satiate its passing.

As soon as I stood up this morning, none of the blood in my body followed, and I knew I was off to a troubling start. I had to find a job, as I did the day earlier and the day before that, but I hadn't gotten around to it yet. As I held tight to the bedpost, waiting for my vision to clear, I remembered seeing ads promoting the Ohio job market. I calculated the odds of me ending up in Ohio. This was about how long it took for the blood to reach my head. *I must be dying*, I thought. *Maybe once Long Beach is under water, I'll give Ohio a try.*

Something seemed too still about the air in my room. It was so quiet that, for a moment, I thought I had never woken up—that I had died in my sleep or was teetering on the edge in a comatose state in a hospital bed somewhere. I leaned forward and listened for the distant beep of a heart monitor. The empty ring in the room made me unsure of how to proceed.

Then it hit me that this was going to be one of those days where I spent too much time in the *in-between*—where I got stuck *on my way* to spending time. Where the walk to the grocery store would take three times as long because of the construction on Tanner Boulevard; where the flower shop on Main would be unexpectedly closed due to the neighborhood arsonist.

Instead of getting to anything of substance, I would end up walking until the sun fell and my ankles blistered. I would end up back home, in the sticky living room, with the two plastic chairs and the TV on the floor, probably collapsing somewhere onto the crunchy carpet and staring up at the popcorn ceiling, while the sounds of Zack heating ramen in the microwave bounced around the kitchen walls, and with my cheek pressed firmly against the floor, I would tell myself—as I do each night—that tomorrow would be the start of it all: I would get the job, find the hobby, meet the soulmate, make the babies, and perhaps, at some point, somewhere in all that, start finding ways to save time and smile and be happy.

After the blood had reached my brain, I felt confident enough to let go of the bedpost. I was pleasantly surprised that I didn't faint. Every year these summers got hotter, and every year Zack said he was going to save some money and buy us an air conditioner. This summer had been sucking the water out from inside me quicker than I could drink it, and I couldn't get ahead. Every time I stood, I wanted to faint, and every time I laid down, I could feel my heart pumping out toward my fingertips. There was a vein popping out of my right temple. It hurt when I pressed on it. *I could be dying*, I thought.

In spite of the impending death, I decided to get dressed. I chose a semitransparent sundress with yellow and orange flowers, but it didn't look right because my skin was turning gray. In the living room, Zack was ripping a bong while incorrectly appropriating Tai Chi. An annual mandatory virtual CPR class played in the background, his camera off and his mic muted. He is a terrible lifeguard, but it pays our rent. I am lucky he doesn't mind my leeching off of him.

Actually, I think he likes living with me. He craves the female attention—in love with the chase but never the woman. I'm sure I feed his ego. And if the trade-off of my leeching is an occasional conversation about the new protein powder he's snorting, then living with him is no skin off my back either. He knows I'll never sleep with him. I've never seen him wash his sheets.

"You look feminine," Zack said when I emerged from my room. I wanted to gag.

"Yeah, thanks," I responded, crossing my legs. Suddenly, I was too aware of my vagina and its proximity to the air seeping out of his nose. He is the worst, but I need him.

We just re-signed our lease for another two years. He is the closest thing I have to forever.

"What are you getting up to, Chiquita?" he asked, his eyes closed, his arms and legs wrapped up like snakes on a branch as he unknowingly slipped out of Tai Chi and into yoga.

My head tilted toward him, pounding beneath Earth's gravitational pressure. I could feel myself sliding away, pouring out from the top of my head into a puddle on the floor, the carpet soaking me up before I knew I was gone. I should be getting "the job," but the problem is that I am a writer, and my parents keep sending me money. This means that I have no skills, and I hate helping people as well as working for them.

I am almost twenty-six, and I spent my twenty-fifth year writing about aimless, ashamed, lonely, sex-deprived (but fiercely independent!) young women. I gave them all different names, or sometimes no names at all, and I pretended they were not anything like me. I submitted their stories to various magazines, and no one wanted them, but I grew to love these women nonetheless. I loved them more than anyone I've ever known in real life. More than myself, and my parents, and my sister. Some of them even broke my heart once or twice. I won't name names.

Unfortunately for me, writing fictional stories about women who are nothing like me is not a skill set that can be easily applied to laborious pursuits or listed on a resume. This means that I still need to get the job so that I can acquire the hobby, and fall in love with the soulmate, and curate the babies, and start to save time, and smile at everything, and become happy happy happy happy.

Eventually, in response to my silence, Zack popped an eye open, sending me back into the living room, where his nose-breath saturated the air between my thighs. I squirmed out of his line of vision.

"I'm going to buy some cigarettes," I snapped, and I made my way to the door. In the hall I could hear him yell something, but I was already too far away.

***

I stopped smoking six months ago. It was the last of my habits to kick, but it will be the first I return to when given the urge to relapse. I took up smoking in high school because I liked the way a black iced coffee and a Marlboro 27 looked at lunchtime.

Even at a younger age, smoking was always a peculiar fascination of mine. When I was a toddler, my aunt would take me to the park, and I'd spend the time picking up cigarette butts instead of playing. My older sister would watch me from the top of the slide, grimacing, like she couldn't believe God had given her one of the broken siblings. But even at that age, I think I was onto something. I would have been too young to understand it then, but now, in my mid-twenties, it is crystal clear. Smoking is an excellent way to spend time.

Although I didn't have much of an urge to relapse on anything in particular, watching Zack contort his body into gross vertical positions made me realize that returning to smoking would be a worthwhile sacrifice to make in the meantime. I told myself that the job, the hobby, the soulmate, and the children would have to wait because *smoking was going to be an excellent way to spend time.*

It took me forty-five minutes to get to the smoke shop because the straps on my flats started digging into my ankles, and I had to stop every five minutes to readjust them. Then the traffic light wasn't working at the intersection off of Myrtle and Del Prado, so it took me seven minutes to safely cross. The first smoke shop I made it to was closed. Someone had shattered the glass window. There was caution tape carelessly draped over the shards of debris. At the second smoke shop, they were out of 27s, so I bought Turkish Royals and a boring brown lighter. Despite the faltered journey stripping away much of my energy, I remained no less enthused over the ingenious way I had decided to fill the day.

For the next three hours, I wandered around Seal Beach chain-smoking cigarettes and tossing the butts into the cracks on the sidewalk. I laughed over how uncoordinated I had become at stomping out the lit end of the cigarette. I used to be good at it—timing the flick of the cigarette with the step of my foot so that the rhythm of my stride could carry on without delay. I was like a toddler all over again, but in reverse. Now I decorated the streets with the little yellow filters. Little yellow filters that would take fourteen years to disappear. If I smoked enough of them in succession for long enough, I could leave a trail that would last forever.

***

I threw up on the walk back because I ended up smoking two-thirds of the pack. As I spit into the watery vomit, waiting for more to come, the smell and color of it reminded me of all those yellow filters I left littered on the beach. Soon enough, guilt was washing in alongside the waves of nausea, so on the rest of the way back, I told myself I had to pick up every piece of trash I could find.

As it turned out, I was very good at picking up trash. I found a plastic Target bag to carry it all, and I strategized how to consolidate. I stuffed Kit Kat wrappers into Gatorade bottles and smaller Dorito bags into one larger Tostito bag. I found an oven mitt, which I wore to pick up the needles, and a rubber glove, which I used for anything soggy.

I expected picking up so much trash to have made me weary. But instead, it elicited a strange kind of mania. I yearned for perfection. I wanted the streets to look perfect. I thought about how there must have been a time when they were perfect, and how the passing of time and the influence of bad people must have made them ugly. It made me wonder whether forever was suited for everything.

By the time I got home, the Target bag was filled to the brim, so I went straight to the back to toss it in the dumpster. When I lowered the lid, the dark pink color of the sky in the distance startled me. It was already evening. Night had fallen so effortlessly. I felt I had the trash to thank.

Later that evening, I laid on the floor and stared up at the popcorn ceiling and listened to Zack making ramen in the kitchen, just as I anticipated, but the stuck feeling I had predicted from spending too much time in between spending time was not there.

Maybe I should be a garbage man. My eyes scanned the watermark that stretched across our ceiling from the leaky bathtub in Linda's unit.

Trash lasts almost forever, I thought.

Maybe tomorrow I will wake up and get a job at the dump, and become a recycling hobbyist, and marry a garbage collector, and make dozens of garbage babies, and live amongst the trash, and save time to save time just to save time, and smile too much, and become disgustingly, disgustingly, disgustingly happy.

"Me and You (and Everyone Else)" was previously published in *Cult Magazine*.

"Willie" was previously published in *Currant Jam*.

Ackowledgments

I'd like to thank Amy Sewell, Geo Bradley, Frankie Whitty, Patrick Ford, Cecily Pierce, Matt Wyeth, Eva Gonzalez, Christian Jarod Vitug, Chaire Louise, Blair Reynolds and Ollymandias for their part in helping me make this book. I would also like to thank Jacqueline Schaeffer, Logan Andrews, Natasha Camirand, Amir Kashfi, Nykolle Sarabia, Kevin Goodman, Camdon Blount, Raquelle Sewell, and Charlie Sewell for their unwavering support.

SAMANTHA SEWELL is an award-winning film and literary writer. *There Is No Escape.* is her first published book. Samantha's film work has received recognition from The Alfred P. Sloan Foundation, the Ron A. Baham Memorial Fellowship, the Gilbert Cates Fellowship, BlueCat Screenplay Competition, HollyShorts Film Festival, and Final Draft Big Break. Her fiction and prose has appeared in *Cult Magazine*, *Currant Jam*, and *FEM Newsmagazine*. Raised in New York City, she currently resides in Los Angeles.

Printed in the USA
CPSIA information can be obtained
at www.ICGtesting.com
CBHW022306261024
16400CB00038B/735

9 781739 639334